Chapter 1
C. E. S.

85-86

S0-ARP-751

W9-CKK-862

I CAN LICK
30
TIGERS Today!

And Other Stories

I CAN LICK 30 TIGERS Today!

And Other Stories

By Dr. Seuss

Random House · New York

For Audrey

Copyright © 1969 by Dr. Seuss. All rights reserved under International and Pan-American Copyright
Conventions. Published in the United States by Random House, Inc., New York, and simultaneously in
Canada by Random House of Canada Limited, Toronto.

This title was originally catalogued by the Library of Congress as follows:
Geisel, Theodor Seuss. I can lick 30 tigers today, and other stories, by Dr. Seuss.   New York, Random
House [1969]   Three stories in verse: "I Can Lick 30 Tigers Today," "King Looie Katz," and "The
Glunk That Got Thunk." [1. Stories in rhyme]   I. Title.   PZ8.G276Iac   811'.5'2   [Fic]   71-86940
ISBN: 0-394-80094-X (trade hardcover)   0-394-90094-4 (library binding)   0-394-84543-9 (trade
paperback)

Manufactured in the United States of America   3 4 5 6 7 8 9 0

I can lick
thirty tigers today!

Well...
Maybe twenty-nine.
You!
Down there!
With the curly hair.
Will you please step out of the line.

I can lick

twenty-nine tigers today....

Well...
That's sort of
A mean thing to do.
I'll cut down my list.
First group is dismissed.
I'll beat up the next twenty-two.

I can lick
Twenty-two tigers today....

Well...
Maybe I'll lick thirteen.
You! In the front row.
You're excused! You may go.
Your fingernails aren't very clean.

I can lick
Thirteen tigers today....

Well..............................

Quite a few of you seem underweight.
It's not fair, after all,
To lick tigers so small.
I think that I'll only lick eight.

I can lick
Eight big tigers today....

Well...
You look sort of sleepy to me.
Some of you chaps
Should go home and take naps.
I only intend to lick three.

I can lick
Three big tigers today....

Well…
It's frightfully hot
In the sun.
You two, I'm afraid,
Should lie down in the shade.
You're safe.
I shall only lick one.

I can lick
One mighty tiger today....

But...
You know, I have sort of a hunch
That noontime is near.
You just wait for me here.
I'll beat you up right after lunch.

KiNG LooiE KatZ

Way back in the olden, golden days
(In the Year One Thirty-Nine)
A fancy cat named Looie
Was the King of Katzen-stein.

King Looie was a proud cat,
Mighty proud of his royal tail.
He had it washed every morning
In a ten-gallon golden pail.

"My tail is such a lovely tail,"
King Looie used to brag.
"My tail must never touch the earth.
My tail must never drag."

So Looie Katz made Fooie Katz
Follow him around.
And Fooie kept the kingly thing
From dragging on the ground.

Well, all was fine in Katzen-stein.
The King's tail wasn't dragging.
But one day Fooie looked behind
And saw that *his* was sagging!

"My lovely tail!" he sighed with pride.
"Oh, this will never do!
If Looie has his tail held up,
I'm going to have mine, too!"

So Fooie Katz made Kooie Katz
Follow him around.
And Kooie Katz kept Fooie's tail
From dragging on the ground.

Now all was fine
In Katzen-stein...
Till Kooie's pride was hurt
When he discovered *his* fine tail
Was dragging in the dirt!

So Kooie made a cat named Chooie
Follow him around,
And Chooie Katz kept Kooie's tail
From dragging on the ground.

And so it went in Katzen-stein.
Next, Chooie Katz got Hooie.
And Hooie Katz got Blooie Katz.
And Blooie Katz got Prooie...

...Till all the cats in Katzen-stein.
Were hiking round and round,
All keeping one another's tails
From dragging on the ground.

All proud!
Except for one small cat...

...The last cat in the line.

The last, last cat of all the cats
That lived in Katzen-stein.
A most unhappy little cat
Named Zooie Katzen-bein.

His tail would never be held up.
And poor old Zooie knew it.
Because holding up a cat's tail
Takes another cat to do it.

Poor Zooie got so awfully mad
So mad he could have spit.
But he did a far, far braver thing...

He simply yelled,
"I QUIT!"

"I can not, shall not, will not
Lug this stupid thing around!"
He slammed the tail of Prooie Katz!
He slammed it on the ground.

Then Prooie Katz slammed Blooie's tail
And Blooie Katz slammed Hooie's.
And Hooie Katz slammed Chooie's tail
And Chooie Katz slammed Kooie's.
All tails in Katzen-stein were slammed
Including proud King Looie's.

And since that day in Katzen-stein,
All cats have been more grown-up.
They're all more demo-catic
Because each cat holds his own up.

The Glunk that got Thunk

A thing my sister likes to do
Some evenings after supper,
Is sit upstairs in her small room
And use her Thinker-Upper.

She turns her Thinker-Upper on.
She lets it softly purr.
It thinks up friendly little things
With smiles and fuzzy fur.

She sometimes does this by the hour.
Then when she's tired of play,
She turns on her UN-Thinker
And un-thinks the things away.

Well.......

One evening she was thinking up
Some fuzzy little stuff,
And Sister sighed, "This stuff's all right,
But it's not *fun* enough.

"I've got to think up bigger things.
I'll bet I can, you know.
I'll speed my Thinker-Upper up
As fast as it will go!"

"Think! Think!" she cried.
Her Thinker-Upper gave a snorty snore.
It started thunk-thunk-thunking
As it never had before.
With all her might, her eyes shut tight,
She cried, "Thunk-thunk some more!"

Then, BLUNK! Her Thinker-Upper thunked
A double klunker-klunk.
My sister's eyes flew open
And she saw she'd thunked a Glunk!

He was greenish.
Not too cleanish.
And he sort of had bad breath.
"Good gracious!" gasped my sister.
"I have thunked up quite a meth!"

She turned on her UN-Thinker,
Tried to think the Glunk away.
But she found that her UN-Thinker
Didn't seem to work that day.

The Glunk just smiled and said, "Dear child,
You can't Un-thunk a Glunk.
Ask *anyone*. They'll tell you
That a Glunk can't be UN-thunk.

"I'm here to stay forever
In your lovely, lovely home.
And now, with your permission, dear,
I'll use your tele-foam.

"I call my mother every night.
It gives her such great joy.
She lives nine thousand miles away
And I'm her only boy."

"Long distance is expensive!"
Sister cried. "Get off that line!"
But the Glunk dialed Texa-Kota-Cutt
1 - 2 - 3 - 4 - 0 - 9.

"Hello, dear mother," gabbed the Glunk.
"I hope you're feeling fine.
And don't worry 'bout the phone bill.
It's all paid by a friend of mine.
I've just called you up to tell you
How I love you. Oh, *I do!*
And today I did some cooking
And I cooked some Glunker Stew.
Let me tell you how I did it.
You may want to make some, too.

"You take a cup of applesauce.
You add a pinch of straw.
You drop in fourteen oysters,
Seven cooked and seven raw.
You beat it to a frazzle
With a special frazzle-spade.
Then you pour it in a rubber boot
Half filled with lemonade.
Then you toss it in the mixer,
Where you spuggle it and spin it...

"Stop!" my sister yelled.
"This costs ten dollars every minute!"

"Money? ... Pooh!" The Glunk just laughed.
"Don't think of things like that."
Then he said, "Now, darling mother,
Let me see. Where was I at?
Oh. You take it off the mixer
When the stew is nicely pink.
Then you add a hunk of something ...
Hunk of chuck-a-luck, I think.
Then you chuck in chunks of chicklets.
Then you plunk in seven cherries.
And THEN you plunk in, Mother dear,
Three dozen kinds of berries.

"Now, Mother mine, please do this right.
Those berries that you're plunking ...
Unless you plunk them with great care ...
Will keep the stew from glunking."

"Stop! Stop!" my little sister screamed.
"It's not a funny joke.
My father can't afford this call.
My father will go broke!"

"Now, you keep still!"
The Glunk snapped back.
He kicked her in the shin.
"Don't you interrupt my mother
When she's plunking berries in.

"Now, mother, plunk one berry. Blue.
Now, plunk one berry. Razz.
What's that? . . . You have no raspberries? . . .
Oh, everybody has.
But, if you don't have berries, razz,
A Schnutz-berry will do.
You have a Schnutz. I know you have.
Now plunk it in the stew. . . ."

And he went on talking berries
With his dear old darling mother.
He jabbered and he blabbered
One whole hour. And then another!
He talked three hundred dollars' worth.
My sister shook with fright.
"This Glunk might cost us millions!
He might jabber on all night!
My father will be ruined!
We'll be penniless! We're sunk
Unless I can Un-thunk him.
Oh, I MUST Un-thunk this Glunk!"

And that is how I found them.
She was standing there UN-thunking
...The Glunk still talking Glunker Stew...
That Glunk was not Un-glunking!

Could she Un-thunk the Glunk alone?...
It's very doubtful whether.
So I turned on MY Un-thinker.
We Un-thunk the Glunk together.

Then I gave her
Quite a talking to
About her Thinker-Upper.

NOW...
She only
Thinks up fuzzy things
In the evening, after supper.

BOOKS BY DR. SEUSS

And to Think That I Saw It on Mulberry Street
The 500 Hats of Bartholomew Cubbins
The King's Stilts
Horton Hatches the Egg
McElligot's Pool
Thidwick The Big-Hearted Moose
Bartholomew and the Oobleck
If I Ran the Zoo
Scrambled Eggs Super
Horton Hears a Who
On Beyond Zebra
If I Ran the Circus
How the Grinch Stole Christmas
Yertle the Turtle and Other Stories
Happy Birthday to You
The Sneetches and Other Stories
Dr. Seuss's Sleep Book
I Had Trouble in Getting to Solla Sollew
The Cat in the Hat Songbook
I Can Lick 30 Tigers Today and Other Stories
The Lorax
Did I Ever Tell You How Lucky You Are?
Hunches in Bunches
The Butter Battle Book

BEGINNER BOOKS

The Cat in the Hat
The Cat in the Hat Comes Back
One Fish Two Fish Red Fish Blue Fish
Green Eggs and Ham
Hop on Pop
Dr. Seuss's ABC
Fox in Socks
The Foot Book
My Book About Me
Mr. Brown Can Moo! Can You?
Marvin K. Mooney, Will You Please Go Now?
The Shape of Me and Other Stuff
There's A Wocket in My Pocket
Great Day for Up
Oh, The Thinks You Can Think
The Cat's Quizzer
I Can Read With My Eyes Shut
Oh Say Can You Say?